Do Frogs Have Ta

Learn to Read Series
Book 15

Cataloging-in-Publication Data

Sargent, Dave, 1941–
    Do frogs have tails? / by Dave and Pat Sargent ;
illustrated by Laura Robinson.—Prairie Grove,
AR : Ozark Publishing, c2004.
    p. cm. (Learn to read series ; 15)

    SUMMARY: A little tree frog can climb
and jump, but even though he looks and looks,
he cannot find his tail.
    ISBN 1-56763-825-2 (hc)
          1-56763-826-0 (pbk)

    [1. Animals—Fiction.] I. Sargent, Pat, 1936–
II. Robinson, Laura, 1973– ill. III. Title.
IV. Series.
    PZ7.S2465Ic 2004
    [E]—dc21   00-012635

Printed in the United States of America

Do Frogs Have Tails?

Learn to Read Series
Book 15

By Dave and Pat Sargent

Illustrated by Laura Robinson

Ozark Publishing, Inc.
P.O. Box 228
Prairie Grove, AR 72753

Dave and Pat Sargent, authors of the extremely popular Animal Pride Series, plus many other books, visit schools all over the United States, free of charge.

If you would like to have Dave and Pat visit your school, please ask your librarian to call 1-800-321-5671.

Do Frogs Have Tails?

Learn to Read Series
Book 15

I am a tree frog. I am little, and I am green.

I am a little green tree frog.

I have long hind legs. I have smooth skin.

3

I have a skinny waist. I have webbed hind feet.

Can you see me? Do you think I am cute?

I am a cute little frog. I am a cute little tree frog.

I live near water. And I can live in a tree.

Can you see me? Here I am. Look up here.

With my webbed hind feet, I can swim in water.

I can jump on land. I think that is neat.

Look at your feet. Look between your toes.

Are your feet webbed? Are they? Look again.

I have one big problem. I cannot find my tail.

I have looked and looked. Do you see it?

Where is it? I have looked high and low.

It is not on my knees. And it is not on my toes.

It is not on my stomach. It is not on my back.

Do frogs have tails? Do you know?

18